ALEX'S
Adventures
AT THE AMUSEMENT PARK

Eduard Delgado ★ *Francesc Rovira*

Derrydale Books
New York

"Let's play a trick
on the train driver.
We'll start the train and
see how fast he wakes up."

The amusement park is a
fantasy land for children and adults
where anything can happen.

3

The train takes off so fast that no matter
what he does, Alex can't stop it from going
off the tracks. And as they pass by the pond,
the poor driver ends up falling into the water.

"Watch out" Get out of the way! I don't
know how to stop!"

5

The train keep going on its crazy way and ends
up inside the Haunted House. Ooohhh!
All sorts of strange voices are floating through
the air—the voices of witches, demons, and dragons.
How scary!

8

"The balloons! All the balloons are going to float away!" Alex is beginning to get worried. He moves the control levers every possible way but he still can't stop the train.

"Phew! Thank goodness we're out of the Haunted House!"

9

"At least I've got it back on the tracks," thinks Alex. "Besides, the roller coaster is lots of fun and from up here you can see the whole town."

"My doll! My doll! She's fallen out of the train!"

By this time everyone wants to stop
the train—the grandmother, the
policeman, and the balloon seller.
But with Alex driving, it keeps
going faster and faster—to the
great delight of all the passengers.

"My doll! Give me back my doll!"

14

Next, the train races through the snack bar. Oops! That's the end of the ice cream and the sandwiches. And there goes the pretty pink-and-white awning that covered the end of the car.

"Do you think it'll stop if I push these two levers that way?"

Which is going the fastest—the cars, the train, the policeman, the grandmother, or the balloon seller?

"Alex, this is so much fun! Why don't we leave the amusement park and go all the way to the city?"

Finally, by moving the controls this way
and that, Alex manages to stop the train.
While the driver looks over the damage and
the grandmother grabs her grandson, the
policeman gives Alex quite a scolding.

"But it wasn't my fault!
I wanted to stop it right
from the beginning but I
didn't know how!"

ALEX'S FIVE GAMES
AT THE
AMUSEMENT PARK

1. ALEX'S BALLOON GAME

As we go through the book we see 95 colored balloons. The street vendor is holding some, others have been sold, and others are floating through the air. Who's going to be the first to discover them all?

2. ALEX'S ANIMAL GAME

A cat, a parrot, some fish, birds, and ducks are also having fun at the amusement park. All together, the drawings show 34 animals. Can you find them all and name the ones we see most often?

Please keep

386

Published by A & C Black (Publishers) Limited,
35 Bedford Row, London WC1R 4JH
© 1990 A & C Black (Publishers) Limited

A CIP catalogue for this book is
available from the British Library.

ISBN 0 7136 3314 X

Acknowledgements

The illustrations are by Jakki Wood

Photographs by Ed Barber, except for p4, 8, 13, 14, 16, 17, 22,
23(t), British Waterways, p19(t), p19(b), p20(b), Zefa p20(t)
Nederlands Tourist Board

The authors and publisher would like to thank the following
people whose help and co-operation made this book
possible: the staff and pupils of Bounds Green Junior school.
Giles at the Pirate Club, Camden.

Typeset by August Filmsetting, Haydock, St Helens
Printed in Belgium by Proost International Book Production